# KING OF
# BOREDOM

Ilaria Guarducci

**Schiffer Kids**™

4880 Lower Valley Road, Atglen, PA 19310

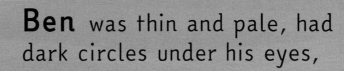

**Ben** was thin and pale, had
dark circles under his eyes,

and never
enjoyed
**himself.**

He had **always** been like that,
as long as he could remember.

His favorite color was light gray.

His favorite dish was plain white pasta.

The sport he practiced consistently was sitting **STILL**.

And when he had free time, he loved staring into *space*.

He was bored **no matter what** the occasion.
He didn't know why; that's just the way it was
and there was no cure.

They had tried to call doctors,
clowns, and soothsayers, but
**nothing seemed to work.**

He was bored
during **ANY**
time of the year.

In **ANY** weather.

IN ANY

POSITION!

He was so **good** at being **bored**
that one day he locked himself in his room
and decided to call himself

# THE SUPREME KING
of Boredom.

And since a king should have at least one t[...]
he decided to build one.

Then he decided that to be convincing he had to have
a **castle** . . .

. . . and then guards on horseback, a servant, and a troop of subjects. All of them, as bored as he was.

And then . . . why not? **A QUEEN!**

He was very satisfied
with his new kingdom.

They spent a lot
of time being
bored **together**.

Every Wednesday afternoon, the guards
organized **bingo for the elderly**,
and the courtesans met to read
**dictionaries, memos, and receipts.**

On Saturdays there was a **big chess game**
(but only one, so as not to have too much fun),
then everyone went to bed early.

On Sundays they all dressed in gray,
ate tarts, and burnt cakes
at a really boring party.

And it was there that Ben felt at the height of boredom, free to fill the void, to feel bored.

But so bored,

so bored,

so bored
that

he almost enjoyed himself . . .